MOONLIT STRANGE

A DEMON WITCH SHORT STORY

KAT SIMONS

MOONLIT STRANGE
Copyright © 2021 by Katrina Tipton
All rights reserved.

Print Edition Published 2023 by T&D Publishing
Cover design: © 2023 T&D Publishing
Interior book design © 2023 T&D Publishing
ISBN-13: 978-1-944600-67-9 (Trade Paperback Edition)

This is a work of fiction. All of the characters, places, organizations, and events portrayed are either products of the author's imagination or are used fictitiously. Any resemblance to actual persons, living or dead, business establishments, events, or locales is entirely coincidental.

First printing T&D Publishing edition: April 2023
Second printing: December 2025
For information, contact T&D Publishing
https://www.tanddpublishing.com

Moonlit Strange

For those who fight their own personal demons
And live to fight another day.

And for my family. Who help me face my demons.

CHAPTER ONE

*A*ngie Jordan let out a slow breath and tried not to breathe back in too deeply. She still gagged. The smell of sulfur and roasting meat coated the back of her tongue with rotten egg flavor, overcoming the more pleasant scents of damp earth, juniper, pine, and oak trees. After two years of doing this, she'd have thought she'd be used to the stench. But no. It still turned her stomach every time.

The ground beneath her was cold and hard, the damp soil leeching through her jeans. There'd be snow in this part of the Sandia Mountains soon. She could practically taste it. Or at least she had before the sulfur stink permeated all her senses. She welcomed the cold. It was a much-needed counterpoint to the heat from the escaped demon standing twenty feet below them.

She wasn't sure how she felt about a demon being loose practically in her backyard—well, at least the mountains east of where she lived in Albuquerque—but it did make returning home later easier than their usual hunts.

Around her, darkness had settled over the woods, which only made the demon's glow seem more intense, a strange sort of moon in the middle of the trees. Beyond the beast's glow, a pinpoint of light from a campfire, just visible in the distance, looking incredibly small and vulnerable.

The area was mostly quiet, all the wildlife vanished ahead of the demon's approach, so that when the demon chuckled quietly, the sound vibrated across her nerves in a sharp sting.

Crouched on the ground next to her, Sebastian leaned in close and whispered, "Almost ready?"

"I found the right tree," she murmured back in his ear so they wouldn't be overheard. His delicious scent helped push out the demon's rotten egg stench so she leaned in closer to him, breathing him in. "I'll be ready when you are."

She shivered at the brush of his lips against her cheek, and her heart pounded a little harder.

Below their vantage on a small ridge overlooking an oak and pine encircled clearing, the beast's red and yellow glow intensified, the lava that made up its skin starting to swirl. It had spotted its prey.

The creature hadn't even pretended to be anything but a demon. Most freed demons shapeshifted to the form of a human, or took over the body of a human, depending on the species. This one, newly freed and still stinking of its own realm, hadn't bother. It stalked through the trees in its melting lava form, shaped roughly like a human but with giant, curved horns on its head, hooves for its feet, and towering over an average human at nearly ten feet tall. Its eyes were a black so dark they looked like bottomless holes in its otherwise glowing face. And its mouth was filled with sharp sharp teeth.

The Fire Beast was such a classic, stereotypical image of a demon, she almost understood why it didn't try to hide its natural form. Watching that creature approach would send any human into a screaming state of terror, a flavor all demons savored.

And it was hers and Sebastian's job to banish the beast back to a demon realm so it couldn't kill again.

"I'll get between it and the campsite," he murmured, his English accent harder to detect when he whispered. "Will that give you enough room to work?"

She nodded. "That tree?" She pointed to the left and a few feet in front of the demon without actually looking at the tree in question. "That's the one. Aim for that."

"Stay safe," he said and this time kissed her on the mouth.

When he leaned away, she took one last moment to study his gorgeous face, his dark eyes bright in the demon's strange glow, the hint of red in their depths stronger as the fight approached. A trickle of sweat rolled down his dark temple, and she wondered at him allowing that. He was a hunter. He could will himself not to sweat.

She touched his cheek. He needed a shave.

"Stay safe, too," she murmured.

He winked and eased back, his movements surprisingly quiet for such a large man. But he was a demon hunter, with the will to fend off creatures most humans only thought about in nightmares. When you could will your blood to flow like molasses through your veins and will your own heartbeat down to almost nothing, moving quietly over the uneven ground, avoiding branches and dried leaves, was simple.

She fingered the pentagram charm on her

bracelet, letting the familiar pattern press into her fingers even as her adrenaline surged.

She waited to move until Sebastian stepped from the darkness into the demon's path. The lava glow from the beast washed across Sebastian's dark skin, the weird illumination like red moonlight, a color that intensified the red tint in Sebastian's eyes.

A piercing burst of drunken human laughter filtered through the clearing from the distant campsite.

The beast chuckled, low enough to make the ground shiver. "You cannot stop me, tiny hunter," it said to Sebastian. "I am all powerful."

Angie picked that moment to scramble back down the hill, making her way to the tree she'd pointed out to Sebastian. She kept the two in sight, as much as she could, while creeping inside the treeline. Staring at them meant she would know in an instant if Sebastian was in trouble, but it also kept her from inadvertently looking at any of the surrounding trees before she was ready.

"Demons always say shit like that," Sebastian said, his accent rolling the words with a hint of Manchester. "And it's always a bluff." He pulled a large wooden cross from the thigh pocket of his canvas pants and held it in front of the beast.

"Now it's time for you to return to where you came from."

"You think that symbol will work on me?" The demon sounded amused, but it took a step away from Sebastian.

Sebastian smiled. "You escaped a man who used this religion's symbols to call you. That makes you vulnerable to the symbols." He moved a few feet closer to the demon.

The Fire Beast straightened to its full height and held its position until Sebastian was within reach, then it snarled and stepped back another few steps.

"That won't banish me," the demon hissed. "I am free. I will feed and stay free in this realm filled with so much easy prey." A long tail, tipped with a wicked looking spike, unfurled behind the demon, and black wings that hadn't been there earlier rose above the beast's shoulders. "You can't stop me, little hunter."

"We'll see," Sebastian said.

Angie reached the tree she'd been aiming for but continued to keep her gaze on the demon and the hunter. She had to time this just right, or the beast might escape.

She'd already enclosed the distant human campsite in a protective circle, and because the campers were a little drunk, they'd thought having a real-life witch creating a magic circle around them was funny. They didn't believe an actual demon was approaching, but they were game for a party. Angie had promised to tell them their futures if they stayed put—and as a touch psychic, she was good at reading people and telling them what they wanted to hear, even if she didn't always get a look at their future when she touched them. So long as the group of humans remained around that campfire, inside the circle she'd drawn around them, they'd be safe.

The problems started when the demons got near enough for humans to see them. Then the humans tried to run away. Always. Running, breaking open the circle, left them vulnerable. And complicated her and Sebastian's task.

After the second time that had happened, she'd suggested they try to banish the demon before it reached the humans it was stalking. Too logical in hindsight.

The Fire Beast made a lunge toward Sebastian, but Sebastian held his ground and raised the wooden cross. The demon's skin flared a bright orange as it came up against the symbol and it hissed, lurching backward.

The power wasn't necessarily in the cross, though because a cross and various Christian symbols had been used to call this demon, those symbols worked against it. The real power, though, was in the will of the hunter.

A demon hunter had to have a will stronger than a demon's. If the hunter's will to triumph faltered, even a little, the beast would win and the hunter would die. Most of the time, the hunters tried to contain demons before they escaped the hold of the human who'd summoned them. Sometimes, they succeeded.

Sometimes, they arrived too late.

Once a demon was freed from the confines of whatever ceremony the summoner had used, it could do as it pleased in this realm. Breaking free cost a demon power, though. They couldn't cut themselves off from their own realm without losing something. The amount of power they sacrificed depended on the demon, the deal they'd made with their summoner, and the way they manipulated a break in that deal. The more powerful the demon, the more they lost to stay here. Most demons who made this move, however, didn't care.

Some hid in human form and just went about their business, escaping here to get away from stronger beasts, to avoid being prey themselves. The hunters usually left those creatures alone. So long as they didn't kill anyone.

Other demons escaped into this realm with the

intention of causing destruction and chaos. Those were the ones the hunters went after.

This Fire Beast had eaten the human who'd called it, leaving behind a bloody stump of leg and a few fingers, the only evidence of the human. The authorities would attribute the murder to a human killer, someone crazy and dangerous. Days would be spent searching for the murderer, all to no avail.

It was better the population as a whole didn't really believe in demons. More might be called into this too-vulnerable realm if they did.

"I will not be sent back," the Fire Beast snarled at Sebastian and lunged for him again. The claws tipping the beast's hands glowed a fierce white.

Sebastian's eyes narrowed against the heat, but he didn't move and he didn't look away from the demon's gaze even as its claws swiped dangerously close to his ear.

Angie sucked in her gasp, holding her warning inside. She'd distract Sebastian if she yelled now. They'd done this enough, she'd learned to keep quiet until just the right time. Still, it never stopped terrifying her when the demons got that close to him.

"I will not be sent back," the beast roared.

And from the rolling lava of his body, it pulled

out a fire sword, the blade made of the same glowing red lava as the monster. The sword was huge, easily six feet long, almost Sebastian's full height. When the demon swung the blade through the air, it made a whooshing noise and flames of light followed in its wake.

Sebastian tilted his head to one side as he studied the sword. "Pretty," he said.

The demon raised the blade high over its head and swung down, the tip of the blade aiming straight for the top of Sebastian's head.

CHAPTER TWO

Sebastian dove to one side, and the demon's sword bury deep into the earth where he'd just been. Angie couldn't help her gasp that time.

The ground sizzled. The smell of burning leaves and pine needles rose into the air, dampening the demon's sulfur stench. A small fire started near the sword, a fire that would turn into a raging forest fire if they weren't careful.

She cursed under her breath. She hated Fire Beasts.

The demon pulled its sword free of the ground and swung it at Sebastian again. Sebastian dove away, then raised the cross. The demon snarled and stumbled back a step. The tip of its sword touched the ground again, sparking another small fire. The demon flicked its tail over the flames, scattering the little sparks to make more little fires. Then it fanned its wings, adding oxygen to the mix.

Damn it.

Narrowing her eyes to focus her concentration away from Sebastian's fight, she breathed out the words of a rain spell, moving her hands in a long-practiced pattern, careful of her finger movements as she chanted. Pulling up her inner magic to aid the construction of the spell, she called on the element of water, focused on drawing the surrounding moisture to a single spot over their heads.

Careful. Careful.

Too much rain and the area would get treacherously slippery. Too little and the forest would burn.

She sensed, rather than saw, the gathering cloud, the pull of precipitation from the air into a concentrated ball, building and building, until with the final word of her spell, the last, long drawn out word of the chant, and a flick of her fingers, the cloud burst and rained poured down over the clearing.

The fires the demon had started smoked and died. The demon's blade dimmed under the wash of water, its outer surface hardening into a black rock. Angie didn't have any illusions that would keep the sword from bursting into flames again, but it was a nice bonus. There wasn't enough water in the area to solidify the demon's body. That would take a storm so big it would be as dangerous as the beast itself. But containing its sword, even for a few minutes would help Sebastian.

And the damage to its sword distracted the demon. It roared and shook the weapon, then bashed it against a nearby tree. The tree cracked, toppling backward in a loud crash of breaking branches and splintering wood.

Angie winced. That tree had fallen away from them, but if the demon decided to, it could flatten the whole area, dropping trees onto their heads. Sebastian might be able to will the trees from falling on him, but she didn't have a handy magical shield that could take that kind of weight.

They had to get the beast back to its realm. Now.

The demon laughed and swung its still hardened sword at Sebastian. Sebastian rolled under the swing, coming up closer to the demon instead of moving farther away from it. He raised his wooden cross, and the demon covered its eyes with its free hand even as its skin brightened orange again.

Sebastian pulled off the base of the cross, revealing a long, thin, sharp knife. He sliced it across the demon's exposed chest and then rolled away from the beast's wild swing, coming up in a crouch a few feet away.

Angie took that as her moment. She braced herself, because this was always the hardest part.

For her.

This next step didn't take magic—in fact, she used the protection spell on the pentagram charm on her bracelet to help her *not* do this too often. It required something other than magic, a dangerous, exceedingly rare—thank the universe!—trait.

And through some very very bad luck, she'd been born with that trait.

She turned to the tree she'd located earlier, the one with its trunk forming a natural V-shape. Not Vs in the branches. Not some pieces broken off to cause that shape. The trunk of the tree had to split and grow out in two directions. She stared into the center of that V…

Seeing the demon realm through it without any effort at all.

Even at a glance, that world was there. Watching the fight between Sebastian and the Fire Beast, she'd been aware of the hellscape realm just at the periphery of her vision.

Now that she looked, now that she *saw* it, the

smells leaked out. The heat. Just around the edges of the tree, she was still aware of the woods, the trees stretching out beyond the one she stared into, unaffected by what she witnessed. The barrier between realms softened. She could feel it getting thinner, weaker. And soon, if she wasn't very careful, something on the other side of that breach would notice.

If they spotted the opening, they'd take it. Spilling into this realm like a plague.

That had happened only once, but it was enough to haunt her nightmares to this day.

She fingered her pentagram, taking what strength she could from the charm, and called out, "Sebastian, now!"

Even to her own ears, her voice sounded deep and loud and not quite her own.

She couldn't turn away from the breach without closing it. As soon as her attention moved off the tree, the barrier between realms would thicken again. The weakness in the barrier would still be there, for her to open again if she *looked*, but nothing the other side would notice or could get through. They couldn't see the doorway between realms from that side, if she wasn't holding it open. She wouldn't have been able to either. There were no trees in this particular demon realm. Just heat and lava and sulfur and smoke. Blackness underfoot. An orange and red sky of fire overhead.

A hellscape worthy of the name.

Sounds from Sebastian and the demon's fight grew louder, and she knew Sebastian was driving the demon this way. She stood to the side but couldn't move too far from the tree or she wouldn't be able to hold open the breach. Still, she hoped there was enough room. Her job, right now, was to hold the rip between the realms open, to concentrate on that and that alone, until she saw the demon fall through.

Then she could look away.

Or at least try to.

Crashing. Curses. The demon's hiss. Another roar of anger. She winced when she heard another tree break and collapse, praying to the Goddess no trees collapsed on her. Praying the demon wouldn't figure out the one way to close the doorway between realms would be to hack off one arm of the tree trunk's natural V. Without that, she didn't see the demon realm beyond. It was out of her reach.

Under different circumstances, she was good with that.

Another distant sound reached her. More hissing. And chittering. Loud and insistent.

Not the chittering.

Not that.

Her heart hammered. The chittering meant more demons were approaching from the other side. Her ears hurt with the sound. Her nerves erupted in pain. Her teeth ached.

She couldn't see them yet, but oh how she hated that sound.

The sounds of the fight behind her got closer, but the tug and hold of the demon realm had her in its grip now. She stared into the hellscape and waited to see the demon fly through.

"No!" The demon's voice, loud above even the sounds of other approaching monsters. "I won't go back!"

"Be gone, demon." Sebastian's voice, deep and powerful. Cutting through the noise in her head. "You will not run free in my realm." His command carried power. Not the power of the symbol in his hand, the knife it had hidden…

This was the power of his will.

Even Angie felt that power, rolling over her. Compelling the demon forward. That strength of will never cease to amaze her. And Sebastian's power gave her the will to hold her place. Not to flinch when she felt the demon's heat on her right. Not to turn away and lose the connection to the demon realm.

From the corner of her eyes, she saw the glow

of the monster, bright now, and very orange under Sebastian's assault. It hacked downward with its sword.

Temptation to check on Sebastian. She ignored it.

More of the demon pushed into her view. One arm raised to ward off Sebastian, the other holding the sword up over its head like a knife, stabbing downward again and again.

Sebastian's voice. "You will not run free in my realm. Be gone, demon." He rolled the words with so much power, the demon stumbled back another few inches closer to the breach.

"Be gone," Sebastian said, louder. Then again, even louder.

The hairs on Angie's arms rose. A chill rushed through her body. She didn't turn away from the hellscape.

The demon roared a denial. Tried to push forward. But the realm had him now. The other side dragged him back, like calling to like, nature righting itself by returning things to where they belonged. Between the call of its own realm, and Sebastian's will to win this fight, the demon didn't stand a chance.

It screamed another denial and threw its sword at Sebastian. She didn't see where it landed, but Sebastian's voice assured her he was still safe.

The beast grabbed at the tree trunk as its realm sucked it in. It used its wings to try and block the doorway. The tree trembled but wouldn't break now. The demon was caught. Stuck inside the opening of its realm and holding it open, even without Angie's abilities.

The fact that the opening couldn't close while the demon resisted its pull wasn't good.

Sebastian stepped into her peripheral view now. "You've lost," he said, his voice still deep and powerful, but quieter now. "Be gone, beast. This is not your time."

"I will not lose," the demon hissed. "I have earned this right to feed."

"No." Sebastian said simply. "No."

The hairs on the back of Angie's neck rose as Sebastian's will washed over and past her. She only felt it this powerfully, so distinctly, in these fights. He used it in other circumstances, but this was when she really *felt* it.

And it was strong.

The demon's wings bent and tore along the thick, black membrane as it was pushed back into its realm by Sebastian's will. It roared another denial. But too late...

It collapsed backward into the hellscape with a sucking, popping sound that made Angie gag.

"Now," Sebastian murmured.

She started to turn away.

A strange voice from behind them said, "Dude, how drunk am I?"

Sebastian turned toward the human with bad timing.

And a long, spike-tipped tail flicked out through the still open breach between realms and wrapped around Angie's ankle.

Pulling her through the V in the tree trunk…

Into the demon realm.

CHAPTER THREE

Angie screamed. She was too surprised to do anything else. She heard Sebastian call her name, but she couldn't focus on that.

Because she was in the demon realm.

Where there were no trees.

She was no longer holding open the breach between realms. It was about to collapse.

The chittering noise of approaching demons got louder.

Panic and horror made her pulse rush so fast, the sound almost overwhelmed the nails-on-a-chalkboard sound of the approaching horde. She could still feel the opening, still see through to the woods beyond, but that opening was starting to shrink.

The Fire Beast laughed behind her. "If I must be here, human, I will have a final snack."

It still had its tail wrapped around her ankle, and it started dragging her along the burning rocks. Slowly. To increase her terror.

She kept her gaze on the breach, terrified if she looked away she'd lose it, even though there wasn't a tree here for her to look through. She wasn't thinking with any kind of logic, just pure animal panic and terror.

Feeding the approaching demons.

She scrambled against the hard, black surface, her skin burning, her nails breaking against rocks that stabbed with sharp edges like glass. She had just enough sense left, around the panic, to summon a spark spell. It wasn't a dramatic spell, but it was one she'd used enough on her brothers as a kid, it was instinctive and ingrained. She didn't have to think about the words, or the twist and flick of her fingers to seal the spell.

A spark of electricity, sharp and powerful, traveled down her leg and buzzed with enough voltage into the demon's tail, the beast snarled and leapt away.

Freeing her ankle.

She scrambled on hands and knees toward the slowly closing doorway. How was it still open? Terror closed her throat. Panic had tears running down her cheeks. She lurched awkwardly, too afraid to even get back to her feet.

The sound of approaching demons, the hiss of the Fire Beast, the sizzle of her skin on the hot rocks, the smell of sulfur and burnt meat…her burning clothes…her skin…

She threw herself at the breach as the demon's tail cracked out again, a whip wrapping around her ankle. She hissed the spark spell again, giving it enough magic to sting her even as it jolted the demon backward. She couldn't think to form another spell, but her fear fed the spark spell, making it more intense and stronger than she normally allowed. She poured power into the electrical jolt because it was all she had.

The chittering grew louder, so loud now, she couldn't hear the Fire Beast over it. The heat of their approach choked her, stealing what breath she had left.

They were coming.

They were here.

And the breach was almost closed.

She'd be trapped. She was too far away to reach the opening. The demons were almost on her.

She repeated the spark spell, over and over, powering it with magic she pulled from her very core, creating a halo of electricity around her that sent anything that got close enough to touch flying backward. On hands and knees, still muttering the spell, her gaze still locked with the shrinking doorway, she made one final lunge.

"Angie!"

A familiar hand reached through the opening, dark and strong, reaching for her.

She lurched up and grabbed Sebastian's wrist as he wrapped his fingers around hers, locking her in his hold. The electricity around her leapt over his skin in blue sparks of light, but the shock of it didn't seem to affect him.

Or his hold on her.

So strong and solid it was like fresh air against her burning skin. She clung to him as the scrambling behind her intensified, the sounds of the demons drowning out all other noise. Except the sound of her thumping heart.

She looked up into Sebastian's face, the intensity of his stare, gripped his arm with her other hand to hold tighter. And with a mighty effort…

He pulled her through the vanishing doorway.

They landed in a heap on the other side, her on top of Sebastian as he collapsed back into the dried leaves and pine needles covering the forest floor. Cool air, the smell of damp, cold earth. Sebastian's warm body under hers.

Angie felt the opening between realms snap shut, heard the cacophony of angry denials and protests from the demons as the barrier solidified, sealing them off from her world. She didn't dare look over her shoulder at the tree.

She buried her face against Sebastian's neck, her heart hammering hard enough she was sure he could feel it. Sobbing breaths weren't enough to pull in oxygen and she started to see spots.

A gentle hand caressed down her spine. "Breathe, love. Breathe. I've got you. I've got you."

She let his words flow into her, beyond her logic and right to her primitive, terrified core. Letting the litany soothe that part of her that was too scared to even allow thought.

Eventually, her heartbeat slowed to a less terrifying speed. The spots cleared from her vision. She hugged him close, the residual terror of what had just happened leaving her weak.

"I've got you," he murmured into her hair.

"Thank you for reaching for me," she whispered back.

"Always."

The sounds of the hellscape had vanished, though the glare and burn of it still crowded her vision when she closed her eyes. As her fear eased, the pain set in, and she realized she had burns, cuts and scrapes, maybe even a sprained ankle to deal with.

None of it seemed particularly urgent just then.

From a few feet away, someone said, "Dude, that was a trip."

She blinked and frowned up at the man standing at the edge of the clearing, still staring at the tree behind her. He was one of the campers, a thin young man bulked up by a heavy coat and a wool beanie pulled down over his shaggy brown hair.

He shook his head, his eyes wide. "I need to give up the drink, dudes."

Angie closed her eyes and started to laugh.

CHAPTER FOUR

She woke screaming. The heat, the sting of glass-sharp rocks tearing her skin, the sound of chittering demons followed her out of the dream.

Strong arms came around her, holding her tight. And reality settled as Angie breathed him in, clearing the memory of sulfur from her nose, took in her surroundings. She burrowed against Sebastian, her fingers going to the pentagram charm hanging from her bracelet. She rubbed the small silver medallion until she could no longer hear the demons right next to her ear.

"Another one, eh?" he whispered after a time.

"They aren't getting any better." She swallowed hard, finally leaning away from him to get the glass of water she'd left on the nightstand, ignoring the mostly empty bottle of Tequila next to it. Though she was sorely tempted. She gulped down the water, letting the cold sooth her raw throat. Raw from the scream or the memory of pain, she wasn't sure.

"It'll take time, love," Sebastian said, sitting up in bed and letting the sheets fall down around his hips.

He was shirtless, all heat and muscle and strength, a faint glow lighting his dark skin from the moonlight streaming in through the open curtains. And she wanted so badly to just collapse back into his arms and pretend nothing was wrong.

But everything was wrong.

Most of her injuries had healed. The worst of the burns were now just red lumps of healing skin. She could put weight on her ankle again.

But the psychological damage of nearly being trapped in a demon realm…

That hadn't lessened even a little bit.

The panic attacks, the nightmares, the terror of what *might* have happened were almost worse than the actual horror in the moment. Imagining what could have been—the torture, the pain— even now that she was fully awake, those thoughts left her pulse racing and another panic attack just at the edge of her awareness, waiting to strike.

She rolled out of bed instead of rolling into Sebastian, avoiding his arms when he reached for her. She shivered now that she wasn't enveloped in their warm bed, under warm blankets. She snatched her terrycloth robe off a nearby chair and wrapped herself up in it, trying to keep the cold from settling into her bones.

It didn't feel any better than the sizzling heat from her nightmare had felt.

She curled herself up into the chair that had held her robe and set her chin on her knees as she stared across the space at Sebastian. Holding his gaze was hard. She didn't want to do this. She'd been thinking it for weeks and avoiding the decision. Her heart broke and her throat clogged up on the words.

But things weren't getting any better. And they wouldn't as long as nothing changed.

Oh but the pain of what she had to do… Damn the demons anyway. Damn them for giving her this and then forcing her to leave it.

She said the words that ripped her world into tiny pieces. "This isn't going to work."

He nodded, but his eyes narrowed. "You can't come with me on hunts anymore."

She wanted to cry. "More than that. I can't… I can't have anything to do with the demon world anymore." When he didn't respond, she forced herself to say the thing she didn't want to say aloud. "Anything. I can't…" She swallowed hard and rushed on, her words spilling out. "We can't be together anymore. I'm going to move."

"Albuquerque's your home. Your family's here. Where will you go?"

She didn't miss that he skimmed over the part where she said they had to separate. Was he accepting or avoiding? "I have a friend in New York. She works at a place where I can get a job pretty easily."

"Reading cards and telling people what they want to hear," he snapped.

And there it was. The pain and anger. She supposed that was better than indifference. "Yes," she said. "I'm good at reading people and helping them."

"Then go be a counselor," he said. "You're better than some sideshow freak reading fortunes."

"You know that's not what I do," she said, her voice dull. She couldn't even get angry and fight back. She didn't have the heart for it.

She'd just shattered her heart.

He threw off the blankets and stood, pacing through their bedroom in his boxer shorts, his muscles flexing as he moved, his jaw tight under his night stubble. No gray in the black, not yet.

Maybe not ever if he didn't want it. A silly thought at such a time. She was working overtime to distract herself.

"You don't have to do this," he said, facing her, hands on his hips, the moonlight at his back. "Not go this far. You know you don't."

"Sebastian…" She looked away because looking at him hurt too much. "I love you. But your life, everything you are is wrapped up in being a demon hunter. You go where you're needed. And you are needed. I can't stand in the way of that." She met his gaze long enough to say, "And you can't walk away from it either."

Which was true. Demon hunters didn't quit. They wouldn't *be* hunters if they weren't strong enough for the job, at least not for long. Hunters who weren't strong enough died. No one quit. No one retired. She wasn't even sure they could. The urge to go where a demon was overwhelmed Sebastian when it came on him. And he went. Almost like a trance, except he was aware of what he was doing. The instincts took over. He could no more end those instincts than he could stop the blood flowing through his veins.

She almost laughed—a nervous, mildly hysterical reaction—when she realized that because of his will, he actually could stop his own blood flow if necessary, or at least slow it substantially. But he couldn't ignore the call of the hunt.

She could tell by the way his shoulders drooped he knew she was right about that last at least. "You will continue to hunt," she said. "As is right. You're good at it, and I'm not asking you to try giving it up. That wouldn't be good for anyone. But this world of yours… I don't belong in it."

"You were made for it or you wouldn't be able to do what you do," he said, his voice quiet, deeper with his emotions.

"If I were made to be a hunter, I would be one. I'm not. I don't have the will for it. I'm a witch. I'm called to that life. My powers, my strengths bend that way." She shook her head. "And I can't keep pretending I'm able for this path, just because I don't want to give you up."

"You're upset because of what happened. It's still raw. Give it time."

"That's what I'm doing. Time. Maybe even some counseling of my own." Though what the hell counselor she'd be able to talk to about nearly getting stuck in a demon world… She supposed there had to be someone in the magical community who could help.

"Ending our relationship isn't necessary," he said. "Moving across the country isn't necessary.

You can recover here. I can help. When I'm not hunting, I can be here for you."

"And every time I look into your eyes, into eyes I love, I will see that red deep in the depths of the brown. And I'll remember all of it. I can't get past it when I'm continuing to look into it every day."

His jaw so tight she thought he might break a tooth, he spun away from her, cursing under his breath. He ran his hands over his head, over his short, tightly trimmed dark curls. Then made fists against the back of his neck.

She stayed where she was, watching him. Swallowing her desire to take back everything she'd just said and stay. She'd been swallowing this conversation for weeks. Hoping she'd get better. Hoping she'd find another solution.

She couldn't pretend anymore. Even as she watched him start to pace again, the nightmare images of the demon realm taunted her, her imagination calling up all the horrors that could have been. The only thing that had been good in that moment was seeing his hand thrust through the breach, reaching for her, pulling her out.

But what if he'd been a moment slower? What if she hadn't gotten to him in time? What if the demons had broken through her spark spell? She'd been surrounded. Terrified. Too panicked to recall any other defensive spells.

And the demons had been hungry.

She felt her panic rising again, sweeping through her in a blood pounding rush, and she had to put her head between her knees to keep from hyperventilating.

Damn it, damn it, damn it. Why? Why couldn't she control this so she could stay?

The soothing weight of his hand on her upper back only made things worse because his touch made her feel better. Tears leaked down her cheeks.

"I can't do this, Sebastian," she murmured as another sob took her. "I have to get some distance. I can't recover here. Like this." *With you.*

He pressed his lips to the back of her head, then set his cheek against her hair. "I can't let you go forever, Angie. I can't face that. I'd give up everything else first."

She raised her head to protest but he quieted her with a finger across her lips.

"But I will give you time and space. For now." He cupped her cheek. "When you've had time to recover, to get some perspective, we'll come back to this conversation."

"And what if I can't get past this? What if I can never come back?"

He held her gaze for a very long time. The moonlight played funny tricks, making the red glow in his eyes more obvious, giving the scene a strange sort of ambiance that only made her ache more.

"I can't consider that possibility," he murmured finally. "I don't want to. But I will deal with it if that's your decision. I just need you to keep open to the idea that this isn't the end for us."

She didn't want it to be the end either. She couldn't see a way around it, but she didn't want to think this was their last conversation, their last night together. So she nodded, and kissed him.

And in the morning, she packed a bag, got in her car, and drove to New York. Without looking back.

She didn't stop crying until she hit Ohio.

Okay, my romance reading people, don't panic! I promise there's more to Angie and Sebastian's story. This is just the start. Although, for those of you who like tragic endings, you might want to stop reading now. LOL. For those more romantic souls, read on for an excerpt from the first novel in Angie's main series. Bone Lantern Witch, book one in the Demon Witch series, out now.

Angela Jordan is first introduced in my Cary Redmond urban fantasy series, as one of Cary's best friends. If you haven't read the series yet, and would like to, start with the novel The Trouble With Black Cats And Demons. You can read an excerpt from that book following the Bone Lantern Witch excerpt.

Thanks for reading *Moonlit Strange*! For more

on my urban fantasy and paranormal romance stories, visit me at my website or join my newsletter for up-to-date information on new releases, ramblings about books, baking, and balcony gardens, and the occasional free read. There's also two exclusive short stories available for new subscribers—one from my Tiger Shifters paranormal romance series and one from the Cary Redmond series. Both are only available via the newsletter. *Mate Run,* from the Tiger Shifters series, is a very very sexy short story. You have been warned.

Thanks again for reading!

~Kat

KAT SIMONS

Bone Lantern Witch

BONE LANTERN WITCH

A DEMON WITCH NOVEL

EXCERPT

CHAPTER ONE

$\mathcal{A}$ngela Jordon fingered her pentagram bracelet and stared at the natural V-shape formed by the split trunk of the small oak tree. She'd tried not to look, had managed to avoid looking on accident for years. But this tree sitting innocuously along the path from the Mosholu entrance in the New York Botanical Gardens had caught her off guard.

Or maybe her guard was down because of why she was here.

She rubbed the dangling silver pentagram charm in slow clockwise circles, pressing into the pattern with each pass over the top of the dime-sized disk. She took a step toward the tree. A slight tremor from the charm stopping her. The scent of sulfur and heat burned her nostrils, a sharp contrast with the cool autumn air. Ordinary, mundane humans walked behind her on the paved path, ignoring her, unable to see the horror she watched between the oak's trunk.

They were all so luckily innocent, she thought, as a demon from the hellscape noticed her.

She froze. Even her fingers stilled on the pentagram. Her heartbeat pounded. Panic she hadn't felt in months rushed through her blood stream.

If she could just stay still enough, maybe it wouldn't realize she could see it, maybe it wouldn't know.

The creature swiveled its head and flicking the air with its forked tongue, its red-eyed gaze narrowing. Its skin was the color of rolling volcanic lava, hard sections of black covered its chest and thighs, under that a luminous red and yellow glow. It hissed, though she couldn't hear the sound yet, revealing rows of shark-sharp teeth.

She tried to swallow without making any movements, not while it was looking at her. She failed.

The demon raced across the burning, charred land. Charging her. Barreling toward the rip she'd created between its realm and hers. It ran on all fours, even though it was vaguely human shaped, its spiked tail high behind it.

A lesser fire beast. Not the same species exactly. Not the same one as that night.

But the same hellscape.

The same realm.

She held her ground, unable to move even if she'd wanted to, glued by panic and fears she'd worked for almost two years to overcome. The stink of sulfur intensified, along with the burning smell of oak. Ash coated her tongue. An illusion she couldn't ignore.

The demon hit the tree and reached through the split in the trunk, grasping hands tipped with impossibly long claws stretched toward her. She could hear its screams now, so high-pitched the sound ripped across her nerves, piercing and sharp. Its mouth stretched and distorted with its cries, taking shapes no being of this realm could manage.

Laughter and the chatter of a child moved behind her. The real world. Oblivious to the nightmare trying to reaching them. They'd see it if it got out, if any of them escaped. The humans would see it.

And they'd know she let it free.

Angie folded her hand around her pentagram charm, encompassing the white beads of the bracelet itself where it hung loosely around her wrist. The charm burned coldly in her palm, the sensation a reassuring jolt of reality and sanity. A soft breeze moved through her hair, ruffling the baby hairs on her forehead, making her hanging moon earrings tinkle lightly.

Unless she was working, she didn't wear the stereotypical trappings of a psychic and witch. Not what mundane humans expected. No flowing skirts and excessive silver jewelry. No braids or patchouli-scented perfume. Today, she wore her comfortable camouflage—jeans and a t-shirt, hiking boots and a light autumn jacket. Only the pentagram bracelet, which she never risked taking off, and the earrings—a present from her brothers to represent her love of astronomy more than her witchy gifts—even hinted at her lineage.

None of it revealed her most horrible of skills.

The sounds of the demon's screams got louder, a hissing and screeching that raised the hair on her arms. Behind it, more demons noticed the breech. Noticed her. They piled against the thin barrier, pushing through the V made by the oak's trunk like a writhing mass of snakes about to spill into this world.

A tug on Angie's jacket made her breath catch. She sucked in cool air, swallowed her screech, and glanced down.

A little girl, maybe five or six years old, looked up at her with wide eyes and a shy smile.

Angie heard the screams of protest from the oak clearly now, the sounds piercing her skull. She smiled at the little girl in her unicorn t-shirt and pink ballerina skirt. The gold plastic crown tucked into her tightly curled black hair glittered in the autumn sunlight.

When the girl tugged Angie's jacket again, Angie bent lower so she was eye level with the child, moving her big purse to one side so it wouldn't get in the way.

"Are you a supermodel?" the girl asked, her whisper not very quiet.

Angie chuckled. "No," she said. "Are you?"

The girl giggled and bounced on her toes. "I'm gonna be," she confided. "But right now I'm a princess."

"Yeah you are," Angie said. "And a beautiful one at that."

The girl's mother spotted the conversation and hurried over. "Sorry," she said. "I hope she wasn't bothering you. She's convinced you're a model."

"No problem." Angie waved to the girl as her mother pulled her up the paved road toward the children's section of the gardens.

The scent of sulfur had faded, leaving only the faint spoiled-egg taste of it in Angie's mouth.

She glanced at the oak from the corner of her eye, not making the same mistake she'd made earlier. She could still see the faint glow of the hellscape beyond, but the barrier had hardened. No demons would be climbing through today.

She pushed her hair out of her face, letting the breeze cool the sweet at her temples. Then she tugged her jacket sleeves down, covering her bracelet, though she curled her fingers up into the sleeve to brush the charm one last time. She settled her purse at her hip, straightening the strap over her shoulder and across her chest.

Then, letting the fresh scents of green grass, damp earth, and the faint smell of hot sauce from the food truck at the front of the gardens clear out her senses, she moved on, studiously ignoring all the natural Vs formed in the trunks of trees.

ANGIE MET HIM AT THE PAVILION IN THE decorative conifers section of the gardens. Here, dozens of varieties of pines filled the rolling hills, scenting the air. Angie loved conifers. Very few of them grew with split trunks.

"How many times do I have to tell you I'm not doing this anymore," she said as she approached the loan man sitting inside the gray stone pavilion.

The open top let light spill across his face, making him look younger than his almost forty-three years. His short dark hair was still free of any hint of gray, his brown skin smooth, no creases or laugh lines around his dark brown eyes or full mouth. Sometime in the last year, he'd gone from clean shaven to a dark mustache and goatee-style beard, and they were also currently without any signs of gray.

Though, Sebastian was a demon hunter, and they never looked their age. It wouldn't matter if he was forty-three or sixty-three or even eighty-three. Demon hunters remained exactly the age they wanted to stay. They willed away the process of aging the way they willed away demons called to this realm.

A demon hunter's will was an awesome thing to behold. A rare trait in humans, that kind of will. Rarer still that innate skill put to good use. And it was a trait fewer and fewer possessed with each passing year. Still, there were enough to keep the demon realms at bay. For now. It was their job to fight the fights and keep this realm blissfully unaware of the threat.

At least, most people were blissfully unaware.

She refocused on Sebastian. He wore jeans and a burnt orange sweater that served to both honor the season and show off his broad shoulders and strong physique. The color suited him, she thought. Even without the softening glow of the afternoon sunlight, he would look good, though. A gorgeous, stunning man in his prime.

Her chest ached. She ignored it.

As she sat next to him, cradling her overlarge faux-leather purse in her lap, she reminded herself, again, demon hunting was his job. *Not* hers.

He studied her, his head tilted to one side as his gaze traveled over her face, lingering on her eyes, her lips. "You're looking good, Ang," he said, his voice deep, the English accent prominent.

She gestured at the surrounding trees, ignoring the compliment and the way his voice always sent a little tingle along her spine. "The Botanical Gardens was an interesting choice. Unless we're here for a specific reason. Either way, the answer is no."

He grinned, quick and sudden, an expression that gave him a boyish charm. That smile had always gotten her into trouble. "Maybe I just wanted to see you again," he said.

"If that were the case, we could have met for a coffee in a crowded café in the city. No reason to get me out here where no one will overhear our conversation."

"I could have kept anyone from overhearing our conversation even in a crowded café," he reminded her.

"We both know you didn't call me for a friendly reunion." Unfortunately. She swallowed that response. "Or anything else personal. We both know this is business."

In the first six months after they'd broken up, when she'd been determined to be done with demon hunting because it had nearly killed her, he'd come to her several times in New York, trying to coax her back into his world. She'd made the mistake of following him into two more hunts before she'd put her foot down for good. Two more hunts she should never have been involved in after…

She let out a long breath. "I'm not dealing in your business anymore. I can't do it again, Sebastian. I can't."

His smile dropped away. "I wouldn't ask if it wasn't necessary. I don't like putting you through this any more than you like going through it."

She snorted. "Right. Which is why you keep dragging me back in."

She'd been trying to put the demon world behind her for almost two years. She'd worked hard to settle into a life without demons and hunters. Or at least, she'd tried to.

She hadn't seen Sebastian in a year and a half, after yet another hunt went horribly wrong for her. She'd finally, finally demanded he not contact her again unless it was an emergency. The last year and a half had been one of the most peaceful, uneventful times in her life. She'd loved it.

She wasn't going to give that up now, just because he flashed those gorgeous dark eyes at her. No matter how easy it was to fall back into the old ways, the old feelings.

"Ang," he said, drawing out her nickname. He held out his hand, palm up. "I tried to stay away. This time I really tried. But there's no one else like you in this world. And I need your help."

She let out a huff of a sigh and looked out over the trees, keeping her gaze on the solid trunk of a pine just down the hill from them. She'd known, when he texted her out of the blue, she'd known it would be something like this. Some demon related issue.

"No," she said without looking at him. She could still taste the sulfur and ash in her mouth from the earlier incident. That realm… The reminder helped her hold firm.

"No, Seb. No more. Not ever again."

"I told her you wouldn't want to be involved," Sebastian said quietly. "I had to ask."

"Aiden?" Angie shook her head. "Of course."

Aiden was one of the oldest and most skilled demon hunters to walk this realm. No one was sure how old she was, or how long she'd been fighting demons. Just that she was still alive when so many others weren't. She was a legend among demon hunters.

She was also the hunter who'd found and trained Sebastian.

"You weren't her only option," Sebastian said. "Just a more straight-forward choice than any of the others left to us without you."

"I'm not going to ask," she said firmly, still not looking at him.

If she asked what the problem was, what they wanted her to do, she'd be halfway to giving in. She wouldn't be able to hear about the trouble and ignore it. He'd gotten her before with that trick. Better not to know. Better to stay ignorant and let the hunters handle it themselves.

"It's okay, Angie," he said, his voice quiet. "We'll save the child without you."

"You son of a bitch," she hissed. "Son of a bitch." She glared at him, her jaw tight. "I hate you for this."

He nodded. "I know."

"Bastard." She wrapped her fingers around the pentagram on her bracelet. "Tell me."

BONE LANTERN WITCH
Book 1 in the Demon Witch series
Out Now!

KAT SIMONS

THE TROUBLE WITH
BLACK CATS
AND DEMONS

A CARY REDMOND NOVEL

THE TROUBLE WITH BLACK CATS AND DEMONS

A CARY REDMOND NOVEL

EXCERPT

CHAPTER ONE

"Not again." Cary Redmond ducked as another fireball clipped over her head. "You don't think fireballs are a bit over the top," she shouted up at the ceiling then had to duck again as a dagger whispered past her ear.

Close. Her heart pounded. Way too close.

She needed to find the damned cat and get out of here. She scanned the apartment from her dubious cover behind a table piled high with unopened mail. Fireballs, daggers, gusts of preternatural wind, freezing hail, and the occasional lightning bolt dropped around her, roaring through the living room in a bright cacophony of magical mayhem.

The lightning bolts flashing in the small confines were pretty spectacular. If they hadn't been trying to fry her, she might have enjoyed the show.

"Jaxer, I'm going to kill you for this."

Normally, this kind of thing was just a part of her job. She was a Protector and literally got paid to run around keeping people safe, mostly from magical bad guys. Not that she'd asked for the job, but that was another story. It *was* her job, so she faced off against dangerous stuff because the Nags—her bosses—told her to.

Tonight, however, was not an official assignment. Tonight, she was just doing a favor for her demented faery mentor. The bastard knew exactly how to get to her. All he had to do was mention a defenseless little black kitty cat and she was done for. How could she refuse to help a kitty? People did rotten things to black cats on Halloween.

Except Jaxer had forgotten to warn her about the fireballs.

She screeched through her teeth and dove behind the couch as one of the aforementioned fireballs barreled toward her. She cursed Jaxer as she took a quick look under the couch for the cat. Where the hell was it?

She'd called out to it when she'd first entered the apartment but hadn't gotten any irate kitty responses. After her lurching hunt of the living room and kitchen, the only place left was the bedroom.

She pulled in a deep breath as she contemplated the long space of unprotected ground between her hiding spot behind the couch and the bedroom door. Once she found the cat, this would be easier. When she was actively protecting something, very little of the magical dangers could get to her, and nothing deadly would touch her. She just had to *find* the cat first. And quickly. They had to be out of this cursed apartment before midnight. Before the wizard got home and all hell broke loose.

Again.

She ducked flying objects and ran to the bedroom, squealing when a lightning bolt hit the ground right behind her. Crossing her fingers that there were no nasty spells waiting for her, she lunged through the half-open door and cringed in anticipation of magical repercussions as she fell onto a red-carpeted floor. She held perfectly still, waiting. Nothing. She let out a breath and pushed herself up onto her hands and knees, shaking her head. All this for a cat. That bastard Jaxer had a lot to answer for.

She rose to a crouch, trying to calm her racing pulse, and froze.

In front of her sat a huge bed, which she

barely noticed because the naked man lying in the middle of the enormous mattress stopped her heart.

Holy shit.

He was absolutely magnificent. Tanned skin, well-defined muscles, thick, black hair hanging down over his forehead. He was lying against a giant headboard with his head hanging forward so she couldn't get a good look at his face, but his golden eyes seemed to glow up at her from under his brows. Piercing and stunning and breath-stealing.

Cary swallowed. Hard. Because even the captivating gold of his eyes wasn't enough to keep her gaze from wandering over the breadth of his naked chest, the corded muscles of his shoulders and arms, the flat expanse of his stomach. It took a great deal of will power not to follow the line of dark hair arrowing down his abdomen…lower.

The man straightened and Cary heard the clink of chains at the same time as she got a look at his neck—and the thick collar covering most of it.

What the hell had Jaxer gotten her into?

"Who're you?" she asked, breathless and embarrassed.

"Who are you?"

His voice carried a deep reverberation that made her spine tingle. Oh boy.

"I'm looking for a black cat," she said, knowing the explanation sounded inane. Jaxer had told her about Sheldon the Wizard, but this? This was something else all together. What was this guy doing here? He wasn't Sheldon, she was sure of it. But then who was he? And where was the cat?

She blinked and a black leopard lay on the bed where the man had been. She sucked in a sharp breath, blinked again. And the man was back.

"Whoa." Cary swallowed. "*You're* the black cat I came to rescue?"

Oh, she really was going to kill Jaxer now. He hadn't said anything about a fully grown man who happened to be a leopard shapeshifter. He'd made sure she thought she was after a little, harmless kitty cat, not a deadly dangerous big cat who shifted into a beautiful, naked, very large man.

The faery was dead. Not that she knew how to kill him, but that was beside the point.

"Jaxer sent you?" The man's eyes narrowed and his features took on a dangerous edge. He hissed a curse under his breath and shook his head. "Stupid."

"Hey!" She stood, the better to face his gorgeous disgust. No one should look that good while insulting you. "You could have done worse, buddy."

She took a step toward the bed, wiping damp palms on her jeans. The chains she'd heard earlier linked the collar on his neck to the headboard, which was brass and made-up of a scrawl of symbols she didn't recognize but looked like they might mean something if she stared at them long enough. He wasn't bound anywhere else that she dared peek, and the chains appeared flimsy enough. So obviously the power keeping him confined was in the collar.

"What is that?" She gestured with her head toward the thick band of metal.

"A binding ring," he said slowly, as if speaking to a child.

She frowned, both at his tone and the news. "But you just shifted."

"It's been designed to contain both my forms. Any other questions before you get me out of here?"

"Yeah, what crawled up your butt and put you in such a pissy mood?"

"Being held captive for sacrifice by a wizard and having a child sent to rescue me has dampened my day a bit," he said.

She grinned and enjoyed watching his eyes narrow suspiciously. "Child, huh? You know, at my age that's a compliment."

"How old could you be? Twenty?"

She shook her head. She'd actually turned thirty-one last April. But when she got tricked into becoming a Protector at twenty-five, she'd stopped aging at a normal rate. One of the few things about the job that didn't irritate her.

She took a quick moment to glance around the rest of the room. The red carpet wasn't the only gaudy element. Lots of black leather covered the walls and an animal skinned rug, which she was afraid to think about too closely given the captive on the overlarge bed, was tossed across the floor in front of what she thought might be a closet. A wood and metal trunk sat against one wall, red silk drapes covered the single window, and the overhead light was covered by thick, dark metal chains which gave the room strange shadows.

Fortunately, there were no nasty attack spells in here, which meant Sheldon the Wizard didn't want his captive accidentally hurt by a stray lightning bolt. That worked in her favor, giving her time to solve the binding ring problem without being pelted by hail.

Though even if there had been spells in here, now that she was officially protecting someone, she could keep them both safe.

She did wonder why Sheldon would care if his shape shifting captive got hurt before the midnight sacrifice. Obviously, he didn't want him dead. You couldn't sacrifice something that was already dead. But an additional warning spell in here probably wouldn't have killed his prisoner. Maybe. If Sheldon had enough control.

If he didn't, and was as powerful as Jaxer claimed, they really needed to get out of here. Fast.

She eased up to the bedside, still leery of traps, and leaned in close to the leopard man, trying to ignore the yummy, stomach-fluttering male scent of him as she studied the binding ring. It was a thick band of silver and copper intertwined in a complex pattern of twists and turns. Over the silver, tiny runic symbols danced and shimmered so they were nearly impossible to read.

"Oh good," she said, "a hard one."

The prisoner shivered, a low growl rising from his throat. The sound made Cary's heartbeat jump.

Speaking of hard ones.

She could feel his glare on the side of her face, but she resisted looking. She had other things to worry about at the moment.

Like how the hell she was going to get this damned magical containment brace off his neck without alerting the entire mystical neighborhood.

"You did that on purpose," the man snarled.

"Huh?" She glanced at him. "What are you talking about?"

"Don't breathe on me again," he said.

She scowled. "What am I supposed to do? Hold my breath until I get your collar off? Just relax, big guy. You'll be out of here in a minute." To herself, she mumbled, "Wouldn't have gotten this much grief from a proper black cat."

"You some kind of witch?"

"No." After a moment, she sighed and shook her head. "Well, there's no help for it. I'm gonna have to use brute force. It'll take too long to get this off subtly."

"We don't have much time. It's nearly midnight now."

"Gee, really?"

He ignored her sarcasm. "Brute force?"

"Hold onto your valuable body parts," she said and tried not to think about his exposed valuable parts. Then she wrapped her hands around the collar, easing her fingers gently under so the backs pressed against his neck. His skin was warm and another shiver danced down her spine.

"Wait."

She met his gaze.

"What the hell are you doing? If I can't break that with my bare hands, you can't—"

He stopped short when she tugged and the collar came away with a quiet click.

"I'm not without some talent," she murmured.

"Who *are* you?"

"Come on. We have to get you out of here. I just made a lot of magical noise with that little stunt."

"Hold on."

He grabbed her hand. The feel of his warm palm wrapped around her fingers sent tiny sparks of electricity dancing over her skin. He dropped his hold, but she saw his eyes widen with the same shock she felt. He inhaled deeply, and against her will, she watched the strong muscles of his chest rise and fall.

"What's your name?" he asked.

"Cary."

"Cary. I'm Deacon."

"Nice to meet you." Did that sounded as stupid to him as it did to her given the circumstances?

He smiled, a slow, deadly grin that made her pulse race. "Nice to meet you, too."

She blinked and shook her head. "Come on, Deacon. We need to move."

As he slid to the edge of the mattress, Cary turned her back to avoid embarrassing them both —despite the temptation to look over every inch of him. The sound of material moving over skin behind her didn't help curb her less polite impulses, though, so she hurried to the door to see how the lightning bolts and fireballs were doing.

Slipping into his jeans, Deacon watched the woman as she peeked around the edge of the doorframe at the living room and the still popping spells Sheldon had set to keep help from reaching him.

She wasn't the rescue he'd been expecting. He'd expected the damned faery to come himself.

Jaxer had convinced him to let the wizard "capture" him, so they could find out *why* Sheldon was kidnapping shifters. They'd only found a few of Sheldon's victims—their bodies anyway. And they'd been little more than desiccated husks. The rest of the missing shifters... Even their bodies had vanished.

Wizards didn't typically go after shapeshifters for sacrifice. They were too hard to contain, and most of them didn't have the kind of magical energy an average human wizard could absorb through ceremonial magic. Shapeshifting wasn't typically magic. It was just a species trait.

Deacon knew none of the shifters killed so far had had any actual magic. He was a different case, but he was pretty sure Sheldon didn't know that. Jaxer did, which was why he'd come to Deacon in the first place, and Deacon had felt obliged to help even though none of the shifters taken had been leopards.

He suppressed an irritated growl. This was the last time he'd let the faery use him for bait. He'd been chained to that fucking bed all day with no sign of help. Then Jaxer went and made things worse by sending in this…woman to rescue him instead of coming himself. How dare he endanger someone else when this crusade against Sheldon was his own personal business? Bad enough he dragged Deacon into it.

But as Deacon watched the woman straighten away from the doorframe when a lightning bolt flashed, he realized there *was* something about her. He couldn't deny the power she must have to break through the binding ring. Yet she looked and smelled like a normal, human woman.

Her light brown hair hung in long ponytail her back over a battered brown leather jacket. She wore jeans, hiking boots, and a purple t-shirt with a glittery Happy Halloween emblazoned over a maniacally grinning jack-o-lantern. Her blue eyes had sparkled when he'd called her a child, then flashed with irritation when he'd insulted her. And for reasons he couldn't quite understand, he'd found it hard to look away from her, especially when she'd knelt next to him on the bed.

Something about her…something about her scent tugged at his instincts.

Who the hell was she? *What* was she? She had to be more than human, but none of his sense picked up anything particularly preternatural about her. So where did all that power come from?

Jaxer had some serious explaining to do.

Deacon shook off his preoccupation and walked up behind her to stare at the living room over her head. Black scorch marks marred the hardwood floors, and a layer of frost covered one side table. The air was heavy with electricity and the smell of burning ozone.

Despite the multiple magical eruptions, the apartment was in remarkably good shape. As he watched, a dagger flew toward the bedroom, dropped harmlessly a foot from the doorway, and disappeared as if it hadn't existed.

Clever. Less clean up. And a testament to Sheldon's power.

He couldn't blame Jaxer for being worried about the little shit. But given a choice, Deacon would have taken a more…active approach to getting rid of the wizard.

Unfortunately, and he was reluctant to admit this even to himself, his approach probably would have gotten him killed. The bastard wizard was powerful. How Sheldon managed to be so powerful at his age was a mystery. But maybe that was the reason Jaxer was so obsessed with finding out the *whys* behind Sheldon's actions.

If Deacon got out of this apartment alive, he'd ask the faery. In the meantime, he and this very human woman in front of him had to navigate the bespelled living room and get away before Sheldon got back.

Deacon drew in a slow breath and was hit again by Cary's scent. Vanilla and cinnamon. And something else. Something that shot jolts of lust and need through his gut, making him lean closer to her just so he could feel the heat of her skin. He felt a possessive growl rising in his throat and swallowed it back, fisting his hands by his side to keep from reaching for her.

What the hell? He had more control that this. A lot more. He had to or people got killed. Resisting a woman, even one that smelled like heaven, had never been a problem before. With Cary, it took an effort to resist pulling her close and burying his face in her neck to soak up her essence.

If he didn't know better, he'd think she was a witch, casting a lust spell on him.

His nostrils flared. That scent of hers…

It reached down inside him, calling to a deep

instinct. As he breathed her in, his leopard whispered, *Mine*.

Out in the living room, wind-lashed hail whipped toward the bedroom without actually coming through the doorway. And behind that, a lightning bolt sizzled the floor.

"Sheldon didn't make this easy," he said, quirking a brow when she jumped at the sound of his voice.

"Are you dressed?" she asked without turning around.

He couldn't help smiling at the slight panic in her voice. "Yes."

"Okay. Stick close. Stay behind me and don't try to dodge around me. Got it? That's how we'll get out of here alive."

He frowned down at the top of her head. She must have some pretty powerful shields to get through that mess. But she wasn't a witch?

He grunted a noncommittal response, and she swung around to face him. The flash of heat in her eyes made his pulse kick.

"Listen, buddy," she said, her chin tucked back as she glared at him, "if you don't let me protect you, we're both dead. Okay? Don't go trying to be a hero. Just stay close and let me do what I came here to do."

She mumbled something unflattering under

her breath as she turned back to the living room, and he had to fight a completely irrational urge to kiss her.

Over the course of the long day, with no sign of help from Jaxer, he'd had to face the possibility of his own death. His reaction to Cary might be a result of that, a need to reaffirm he was alive.

But as he breathed in the heady scent of her again, he wondered…

THE TROUBLE WITH BLACK CATS AND DEMONS
Book 1 in the Cary Redmond Series
Out Now!

BOOKS BY KAT SIMONS

Demon Witch Series

Howling Dreadful

Moonlit Strange

1-Bone Lantern Witch

2-Spiderweb Witch

3-Storm Shadow Witch

4-Darkling Mist Witch

5-Apocalypse Witch

Urban Fantasy

The Cary Redmond Series

Cary Redmond Short Stories and Collections

Joan of Kerry Series

Friday's Curious Shop Series

Paranormal Romance

Dragon Thief Series

Seven Families: Wolf Series

Tiger Shifters Series

Destiny Cats Series

Romancing the Leopard: A Tiger Shifters-Cary Redmond Crossover Novel

Contemporary Fantasy

Haunts and Howls Collections

**Tombstone Wizard * The Unshattered Sword * Going Out of Business: Everything's for Sale * Anger Management * Demonic Dates * The Museum of Small Art's Everyman * Burning Inside a Stone Circle * Bored Questless * I Just Ate a Bug * Ting Ling * Sophie Saves the World * Black Water Hawthorns * To Dance in Fallow Fields at Midnight * The Troll and the Dressmaker*

Pick Your Genre Collections

Who Steals a Dragon

ABOUT THE AUTHOR

Kat Simons earned her Ph.D. in animal behavior, working with animals as diverse as dolphins and deer. She brought her experience and knowledge of biology to her paranormal romance and urban fantasy fiction, where she delights in taking nature and turning it on its ear. She writes urban fantasy, contemporary fantasy, and paranormal romance in series which combine action adventure, the otherworldly, and a frequent dose of sexy romance.

The newest book in her bestselling romantic urban fantasy series about Protector Cary Redmond, The Trouble with Shifters and Fae Courts, sees a new direction for the intrepid Protector, her sexy leopard shifter mate, and the entire crew. Kat also launched a new novella length Urban Fantasy Romance series that follows the adventures of a magical thief and the dragon shifter prince she just can't seem to shake—and really doesn't want to. The first season of the Dragon Thief series released throughout 2024.

Season Two begins in 2025 with The Crown of Kingship Job.

For something a little different, Kat also publishes fantasy, science fiction, and the occasional hockey romance under the name Isabo Kelly (https://www.isabokelly.com).

After traveling the world, living in places like Hawaii, Germany, and Ireland, Kat now lives in New York City with her family and a library's worth of books.

For more on Kat and her future books

Website: https://www.katsimons.com/
Newsletter: https://bit.ly/KatSimonsNewsletter

KatSimonsBooks
https://www.katsimonsbooks.com
https://www.TheCafeatKatSimonsBooks.com

Social Media
Facebook Page: https://www.facebook.com/
KatSimonsAuthor
BookBub: https://www.bookbub.com/authors/kat-
simons
Bluesky: https://bsky.app/profile/katsimons.bsky.
social
Instagram: https://www.instagram.com/isabokelly/
Threads: https://www.threads.nct/@isabokelly

Join Kat's Newsletter

Stay Up-to-Date

On all Kat's News, Updates, and fun extras

New Subscriber Get Two Exclusive Stories Just for Signing up!

bit.ly/KatSimonsNewsletter

KATSIMONSBOOKS

Mystery

Urban Fantasy

Romance

And More!

KATSIMONSBOOKS.COM